THE WHISPER THAT REPLACED GOD

BOOK II:
SILENT ALMIGHTY

TIMOTHY WOLFF

Partnered with Willow Wraith Press.
Visit our website at Willowwraithpress.com.

ISBN: 979-8-9907730-6-6 (Paperback)
ISBN: 979-8-9907730-5-9 (eBook)

Any references to historical events, real people, or real places are used fictitiously. Names, characters, and places are products of the author's imagination.

Front cover image by Alejandro Colucci
Edited by Jonathan Oliver
Title page image by Coe Lansdell
 Book design by Lorna Reid

First printing edition 2025.

CHAPTER I

THE SCREAM THAT REPLACED A WHISPER

f nothing else, depression was at least consistent. I never had to worry about tomorrow. I never had to worry about today. There was no fear, doubt, no anticipation or dread of any kind. The only thing I felt was nothing. And I felt it with every part of my soul.

Okay, surely you have questions. I will answer some of them, but not all. Not many, if we're being honest. And don't think for a second I didn't see the accusations of "unreliable narrator", "strange liar", "weird silence", or any other of the hurtful phrases hurled upon me by scoundrel readers. For the record: I don't lie to the audience. I lie to myself. If I had to wager, I imagine we are the same in that regard. Here's a quick recap: In my journey to become king, I rambled on for a few chapters about philosophy, eventually obtained my crown, then never felt more empty.

So today, like every other day, I sat upon the throne, passing judgment on the worst of society—mainly Lepock cultists and dust addicts. For whatever reason, both have been increasing in quantity since my reign began. It would have been easier to execute them all. Ironically enough, Lepock would enjoy that. The only time the Silent God ever spoke to me lately was with odd, cryptic passages or a desire to silence the realm. More often than not, I simply ignored him. Not out of spite but apathy. Believe me, if I could silence the realm, we wouldn't be having this conversation.

"State your defense!" General Cyrus yelled at his captive. If I had to guess, the prisoner shivering in the middle of my throne room was a drunk or a dust addict. Too much shaking, and not the type that comes from a brisk chill. Also, that dangerous look in his eyes that basically screamed, "*I will do this again. I will do this over and over because I have no choice. You did nothing to help me and I cannot help myself. The cycle continues. Today, tomorrow, forever.*"

"My...my children were starving, Your Majesty. The droughts have been particularly harsh this summer. I offered praise to the Silent God, but my crops withered all the same—"

"Enough." I sighed as loud as I could to ensure my annoyance was known. What kind of man blames his woes on the sun? It offers life, warmth, and, apparently, an excuse to worship poison. "State your name."

"Yes, of course. Uh, Jacob, first son of Micha, Your Majesty."

"And what is your vice, Jacob? What drives a man to steal from a military commander? If you simply wanted to off yourself, there are more enjoyable ways to end the story."

"Well," Jacob said, fidgeting his feet, "the king's law states that thieves meet the noose, regardless if it's one copper or a hundred gold. Figured I may as well try for the gold."

Some of the room laughed, but that ended when I didn't follow. I had learned there *were* benefits to being king. My silence was infectious, even without having to whisper my favorite word. "Stop dancing with the truth and answer my question."

"I have...dabbled in dust. But, to be fair, addict is not an accurate description. It's been nearly twelve hours!"

Dust. Of course. People who only measure time in hours always have issues. It had been growing worse lately, despite increasing the severity of my punishments. It was difficult to threaten people who didn't care. Ah, Brother Merrick would have been proud. My drug infested brother had been a pioneer in what was to come. Would you think less of me if I admitted to how I missed my family? All of them. Yes, even my father, who had tried to drown me. Part of me still believed that he loved me. Not a lot, but well, to the extent that a father who tries to drown his son can love anything.

I looked over the criminal. My own thoughts brought nothing but sorrow, but at least there was a conduit for my pain. There was a...calm to harming others. Oh stop. Only the guilty ones. I wager you feel it too. Maybe you ran across a man in the marketplace whose voice was too loud. Maybe you simply didn't appreciate the color of his pants. Either way, for a second, a quick second, you considered stabbing him in the middle of his throat. Surely, we all think these things. Such whispers upon the mind is what makes us human. Otherwise, I dare say we would all be monsters.

"My lord?" said General Cyrus, breaking my wagon of thought, which was rather frustrating.

"Oh, apologies. Um...just hang him, I suppose. Is his family here? Charge them one silver for the rope."

To my surprise, the room erupted into murmurs. But why? Was one silver too much or too little? Oh well. If they were unhappy, maybe *they* could try ruling Balewind.

"Mercy!" the captive yelled, falling to his knees. "Mercy, please!"

I didn't bother to rise. I leaned back and said, "Consider my judgment mercy. Despite your worthlessness, despite your failures as a father, I offer you a clean death. You won't have to be here anymore. Some of us would kill for that." To be honest, I was always a bit harsher to the men. It's easy to turn a blind eye to mothers and pretty women. Particularly the ones who looked like Dorothy. Oh Dorothy, it had been so long. Wherever could she be...

While guards pummeled the man for continuing to complain, I closed my eyes and thought back to my joyful nights with Dorothy. For the sake of my average rating on Pleasant Reads, I will spare you the more intimate details but, rest assured, they were wonderful.

"One more, my lord," said Cyrus in a hushed tone, which was a pleasant change of pace. I'll admit, I enjoyed the man. He was a sadist to be sure, but still, he seemed to understand my more subtle attributes. "Not certain about this one. I think she's mad. If not, we may have a situation."

A situation? Oh, I could only wonder! I would take anything to break the monotony of monarchy. And a *woman*? Perhaps it was Dorothy! Perhaps she had finally come to reclaim her rightful place as queen…

The woman approached. It was not Dorothy. I don't know who it was but she wasn't pretty enough to hold my attention. I sighed and slouched back, hoping Cyrus would handle the rest. I was too tired from being tired. Too exhausted from permanent stagnation. Why wasn't anyone speaking? After a bizarre silence, I said, "Well? Someone may as well speak. What are you here for?"

"My…Your Majesty," the woman said, in a rather pleasant voice. On second thought, the fear on her face made her eyes more beautiful. Her nose more slender. Her hair…crimson like a winter sun, little fragments of heaven flowing down like a wave. I could see myself loving this woman. It would take time, but we could eventually grow old together and have three daughters: the youngest of which would grow to resent me as I unconsciously drifted towards more traditional values. In the end, she would be my favorite—

"There is another," she said. "Another…you."

I did not intend to laugh as loud as I did. Strangely enough, the room did not follow. "What trickery do you speak? Another me? There is only one me, and he happens to wear a crown." I tapped my fingers on my armrest. It had been quite a while since

I felt anxiety. It tingled through my stomach, working its way to my throat.

"We heard it," she said. "Or, to be precise, we heard nothing. In all my days, I have experienced nothing like it."

I leaned forward and studied her through my mask. I didn't see any signs of lying. No, it was impossible. Lepock wouldn't bless another. He already had the king. He already had *me*. How fitting. Another to abandon me. First my family, then my lover, now my god.

"Who?" was all I could ask. My voice cracked but my people were smart enough not to snicker. You may think less of me, but my first thought was to snuff out the child. Monstrous? Yes. Practical? Also yes. Perhaps a bit… what's the word…unfair considering my own curse. But if nothing else, and trust me on this: the realm is better off with only one Mute.

"He refers to himself as Lord Deaf. His accent is slightly Southern. While he covers his face in a mask similar to your own, the rumors are that he is quite handsome—"

"Handsome? Well spoken? I would love to meet this prodigal child. Is his crib made of solid gold as well?" I chuckled, and only received a lackluster response from the crowd. They seemed concerned. Hmm. It was becoming apparent that I would have to kill this child, which could be problematic. Listen, I don't consider myself perfect, but harming children is a level of sin that never finds grace. Oh well. I had already entered Eleanor's brothel all those years ago. Heaven did not await me. What was one more sin upon the judgment of angels?

The woman raised her eyebrow at me. Rather rude, in my opinion. "He's not a child, Your Majesty. Tis a full-grown man of twenty-five years."

"Impossible. Silence is not an ability one can hide. My kind were butchered for centuries until I came along." I rubbed my hands together to calm my nerves. Another me? Maybe I had this all wrong. Perhaps we could become friends. Or family! "I shall meet this Lord Deaf. What are his whereabouts?"

"Will…will you harm him?" The girl spoke with a strange conviction. I think she was trying to appear intimidating. To be honest, it only made me desire her more.

It was difficult to answer her question. My natural instinct was to lie, but I didn't know the truth yet. If the past was any indication, I would murder this Lord Deaf. Not because I yearned to, but because all that comes close to my heart, eventually ends up close to my dagger. So I leaned firm and straight, with the honor and decorum of a king who had murdered his own brother. "You have my word, I will not harm the boy. Now, I shall ask again, for the final time: where can I find this Lord Deaf?"

It was unwise for her to pause. Pretty or not, I would only ask twice before choosing a more violent alternative. The silence gave me a moment to realize I never inquired her name. Some habits never change. "In my home. The boy is my son. We traveled all the way from Ganfren four years ago after you legalized speaking Lepock's name. I…cannot tell you the relief that came when the news reached us. It was like an angel had come down and blessed my family. Thank you, King Mute. From the bottom of my heart, Thank you."

Genuine praise was a concept so foreign to me, I nearly fell off my throne. But the time was now. I rose, paused, then descended the stairs to meet her face-to-mask. I laid a hand upon her slender shoulder, pleased at how she flinched. There is a joy to being feared. Power has no quantitative value, but to acknowledge its presence is an unrivaled thrill. And she was right to be afraid. If her son didn't meet my standards, his fate would be an unmarked grave. "Pardon, but I never caught your name."

"Coralie, Your Majesty."

"Well, Coralie, I shall meet your son tomorrow morning. You have my word no harm shall fall upon him."

Looking back, I can only smile at my naivety. Coralie was many things, but still, after everything, I do not believe her to be a liar. I think she was simply…unaware of her son's ambitions.

Unaware her son was destined to become the scream that replaced a whisper.

CHAPTER 2

CLARITY

 h, little one, to which god do you pray to?" I asked.

And, as always, the praying mantis in my chambers offered no response. I had found him—or her? To be honest, I don't know how to determine gender with bugs—in my chambers one evening. Such a strange specimen. One could only imagine how it had scaled my castle walls and found its way here. Like most things I did not understand, my initial response was to solve it with violence, but for reasons I cannot recall, I allowed the mantis to remain. It was one of my more balanced relationships. The mantis wanted nothing, and I had nothing to give. Just two oddities existing in silence. As it should be.

With my meeting with Lord Deaf on the horizon, I was more anxious than I care to admit. The sun peeked through my window and, despite the early hour, I took a swig of my wine. I cannot say if it was delicious. I had drunk so much in the past two years I could barely taste anything. A dangerous game to be sure. What does it say about clarity that its diminishment brings speckles of joy? I dare wager that clarity, not gold, is the root of all evil. Or, at the very least, the root of all sorrow. No one smiles more than a man who knows nothing.

A knock came at the door.

I took a final look in the mirror to ensure I was presentable. Hmm. There was a slight smudge on the bottom left of my mask. I tried to wipe it off but to no avail. That simply wouldn't do. Coralie had said her son also wore a mask. I would *not* get out masked by some Ganfren charlatan.

They knocked again.

"*Enter!*" I said, with more rage than intended. How frustrating that despite being king, I never had any time to myself. Sure, I had total authority over Balewind. Sure, I had the power to decide life or death for my people. But no time for rest. Never any time for rest. At least the anger prevented my voice from cracking. I swear that once you fear the cracks, they always appear at the worst of times.

General Cyrus entered, decorated with medals, pins, and all the other cosmetic rewards that come from years of putting people under the ground. It was strange to see him in full military regalia. He clearly had a different opinion on how this meeting would go. "A fine morning, Your Majesty."

"That remains to be seen." I patted my right side to ensure my dagger was still there, then followed Cyrus out into the halls. "Tell me, and speak freely: how do you see this going?"

"Not well. The mother seemed trustworthy enough, but I worry about the boy. He shouldn't call himself Lord."

"Agreed. And you're certain this meeting should occur in the open? If we must kill the boy, I would prefer to do it quietly."

Cyrus offered a rare smile, reminding me why I trusted the man. Not for his wits, not for his expertise or experience. I trusted the man because he always looked miserable. "A meeting of two of Lepock's chosen ones. In theory, this should be the quietest meeting ever assembled. Regarding open space, well, think of it this way. If you seek to kill the boy quietly, he probably feels the same about you. Kings are never killed in the open. They meet their ends by wine glasses, behind doors, or by very ambitious siblings."

I couldn't tell if that was a slight for how I had murdered Merrick. To be honest, I didn't particularly care. "Fair enough. Any thoughts on the girl?"

"On the who? The mother? She's dangerous. I could see it in her eyes. If the boy dies, she must follow. No exceptions."

It was…refreshing to have someone speak to me so bluntly. Some unsolicited advice to anyone planning on murdering their way to the top: you can fill most of your ranks with fools, but not General. The man who commands the blades should also command a sound mind. But not too sound. That's where it gets tricky. Last thing we need is for the murderer to become the murdered.

I nodded and followed. Even after all these years, it was still awkward to walk the halls I had grown up in. Part of me still checked over my shoulder for Merrick's revenge. Part of me still hoped Mother would randomly appear from one of the corners and hug me. Obviously, neither ever occurred. One of the many prices of becoming king was a severe shortage of hugs.

We stepped outside, and I paused to smile at the sun. The older I became, the more I loved summer instead of winter. Pardon the pun, but there is something about watching people suffer through miserable heat that warms the heart.

"Thank you for coming, Your Majesty," said Coralie. "Your presence honors me."

I flinched at Coralie's perfect voice. I'm not ashamed to admit that I loved this woman. If it pleased her, I would tolerate her awful son. Perhaps one day, I would gift her with another. "The honor is all mine. Forgive me, in our meeting yesterday, we started off on the wrong foot. I assume you know General Cyrus. As for me, no need for fancy titles. To you, I am simply Mute. Nothing less. Nothing more."

I caught her glancing at Cyrus for confirmation. She obviously didn't trust my words. Rather offensive to be sure, but I couldn't remain angry at those eyes for long. "Understood, Your…Mute."

"By all means," I said, "lead the way."

So she did, and we followed. I must admit, since becoming king, I could not recall the last time I had casually strolled through my own kingdom. It was odd, if not unnerving. So many eyes from so many directions. All sorts of stares and glares, all sorts of wacky facial expressions that conveyed fear, bewilderment, or some odd mixture of both. Maybe it was because I could kill any one of them with a quick word. Maybe it was because most of them had never seen me in person before. Or perhaps they simply found me to be dashing.

"Is something the matter, Lord Mute?" asked Coralie, studying me in a matter I could not identify.

"The smell. Or smells, I should say. Are my people too uneducated to bathe?"

She laughed, which was nice, though odd, considering I did not jest. "Most of them have barely enough water to drink. There are very few desires that outweigh dehydration. Particularly in the summer."

"General," I said, "look into this further. Increase the water supply."

"Consider it done, Your Majesty."

Coralie stopped in the middle of the road. "How does one…increase the water supply?"

"Don't overstep," I said. "Enough of this, where is your son? My time is too valuable to spend with vagrants."

I think she was going to respond but thought better of it. She probably considered herself better than me. Imagine that. Superior to a king. Superior to the Silent God's chosen one. The *true* chosen one, not that imposter awaiting us.

If the smells of the marketplace were foul, the side-alley we entered was truly unholy. I had ventured down a similar path once in my youth, when I had been testing out which brothels were the most…enjoyable. I assure you, that had been a mistake.

"Here," she said, pointing to a rundown shack. Surely, she was joking. *This* was her home? The thought of one who had been blessed by the gods living in such filth nearly made me laugh. After a few moments had passed she said, "My home is obviously no castle but it's rude to stare. And wipe that look off your face."

I tapped the side of my mask. "I wouldn't make assumptions on my facial expressions."

"My son wears a mask too. I assure you, I can see through his just as easily as yours." Coralie opened the door then gestured for us to enter. "Royalty first."

"No," said Cyrus. "The meeting takes place outside. In the open." He was right of course, but I *did* want to enter. You can learn much about a man by his natural surroundings.

Oddly enough, my general's words appeared to put Coralie at ease. She took a deep breath, then said, "Good. I agree. But, before I bring him out here, I request—no, I demand your solemn promise. My boy is not to be harmed. Give me your word."

"Consider it yours." I said the words as quickly as possible to make them believable. Again, I didn't know the truth. I had no desire to harm the child, but I had even less desire for the child to harm me.

At the time, I assumed there was only enough room in Balewind for one silent king. I was not wrong.

CHAPTER 3

TODAY, THE REALM SHALL BE ALTERED FOREVER

or the record: Lord Deaf is a stupid name. And before you ask: no, I had never chosen Mute. Most people don't realize that. It had been a joke made by Mother, then it just sort of lingered. Looking back, I don't think anyone expected me to reach adulthood. Probably why they had never bothered to use my birth name, Orion.

I didn't have to ask if the man who stepped outside was Lord Deaf. He was covered in a black robe and a black cape—how original—but the true oddity was his mask. Unlike mine, it was shaped like Lepock, with the wings on both sides and the singular eye in the middle. The image made me shiver. It was simple enough, but more importantly: it was accurate. I assure you, there are no records of Lepock's appearance. I had legalized speaking his name yes, but never approved him to be painted, or worse: carved into a mask. This boy had seen him. Perhaps even spoken to him. Was I staring face-to-face with my replacement?

Instead of bowing, Lord Deaf hugged me and said, "Brother, I have dreamed of this moment for years. We are finally united to spread glory to the Silent Almighty. Today, the realm shall be altered forever."

Was I supposed to hug him back? I didn't appreciate the

familiarity of being called "Brother", particularly after I had murdered my own. But Coralie was watching intently with those pretty eyes. If the path to our love was carved through her son, I would walk this awkward road. I hugged Deaf, then said, "Welcome home." I let go and took a few steps back. "I'm sure you have several questions. In the meantime, care for some tea?"

"After spending a few years here, I care for some answers. First off: where are the statues?"

"Pardon? I don't recall how they do things in Ganfren but we never bother to make statues of our royalty. Paintings, sure, but—"

"I had to craft my own mask when I arrived in Balewind. No one here knows anything about Lepock, save his name. Why is that? What have you done as king?"

Coralie nervously approached her son. She eased a hand to his shoulder then said, "Deary, we spoke about this. Mind your tongue in front of the king. Now is not the time."

"Listen to your mother, boy," said Cyrus, with one hand on his sword hilt.

Oddly enough, the potential chaos made me smile. With his mother upset, I clearly held the advantage. "What have I done as king? Well, for one, you're here. It must have been difficult hiding in Ganfren. I hear they burn our kind alive just to ensure the power is destroyed completely."

Deaf broke free from Coralie's embrace and paraded around like a fool. "Tolerance is nothing more than a coward's compromise. You…you were given a gift. Lepock himself, the Silent Almighty, spoke to you! Despite this, you have done nothing to spread his glory. At first, I placed the blame on the non-believers. But they are only lost thanks to their ungrateful king." The venom in his voice was startling, to say the least. Strangely enough, I admired it. I'm sure quite a few people in Balewind despised me, but they usually did so behind fake smiles and closed doors. To hear someone curse my name with such passion was refreshing.

We were drawing quite the crowd. It would be unwise to kill another one blessed by Lepock, but I'm sure I would rest easier knowing this man was dead. All in due time. A little girl rushed out of the hut and grabbed Coralie's leg, then said, "Mommy? Why is Noah yelling at the king? Are we going to jail?"

"No," Coralie said, going to one knee to hug her daughter. "No, jail. No, violence. Is that correct, Your Majesty?"

I wasn't sure how to feel about Coralie having *two* children. At least there was no ring on her finger. Hopefully, her husband had died or something. "What's your name, little girl?"

"Norah!"

"Well, Norah, tell your brother to behave, and there will be no jail or violence of any kind. You can trust me. I am the king. My word is divine."

As expected, Deaf angrily approached, only to be stopped by Cyrus. Deaf pointed at me, then said, "The only divine words come from Lepock himself. Not some…false prophet."

I sighed. It was growing more difficult to diffuse the situation. This foolish boy wouldn't be satisfied until he was under the ground. I nodded to Cyrus and whispered, "Strike him."

My general swung, but Deaf dodged the strike and countered with his own, knocking Cyrus square in the teeth. It took a moment to realize Deaf was then charging at me. Before I could draw my dagger, he tackled me to the ground, pressing his hands against my neck. I could do nothing to get him off. He was younger, stronger, and filled with a bravado I hadn't felt in years, maybe decades.

My guards removed Deaf and started pummeling him. Coralie's cries were the only reason I felt any need to interfere. The boy was a danger to society and, more importantly: to me. Perhaps Lepock found the whole thing hilarious.

"Halt," I said, fixing the tilt on my mask. "Detain him, but stop your assault. Coralie, I place you and your family under arrest. Punishment shall be determined later." The guards apprehended

Coralie, then I nodded towards Norah. "The girl as well. I am not monstrous enough to separate family."

I ignored their screams, and ensured Deaf was properly detained before I approached. "My only compromise will be allowing your mother and sister to go free after your execution. This is what happens when you treat faith like a dagger—"

"*Hush,*" Deaf whispered, then the world…went deaf.

Or at least I thought it went deaf. Despite the silence, Deaf clearly said, "If my faith is a dagger, then it's the sharpest blade ever crafted. You will know this the exact moment it pierces your throat. My execution will never occur. The Silent Almighty will never allow it."

"What *are* you?" I tried to say, but no words came out. Bless my guards for continuing to detain Deaf. I was clearly outmatched, but at least that simplified my decision. The boy must die. I would hang him for all to see: a not-so-subtle reminder to what occurs when vagrants place their hands on kings.

Deaf tilted his mask, then laughed. "You can't speak, can you? You have no idea what Lepock has given you. Such a precious gift…*wasted* by an ingrate. There is so much power, so much potential in this silence. And all you do is sit on your throne and rot. The winds of change are blowing. Only I can hear them. And like dust, you will scatter away."

I swung and hit him in the chest. If I had no words, violence would have to suffice. I was never particularly strong, but I think fear amplified the power in my fist. Deaf groaned and fell to one knee. I cannot accurately describe how angry it made me to hear that groan. How could he speak? How had he mastered this gift to such an extent? Part of me considered keeping him alive, if only to learn the full extent of my power.

But another part—the part filled with wisdom—already knew the truth: I wouldn't have to worry about who was more powerful if I was the only one left.

CHAPTER 4

REQUIEM OF SILENCE

 couldn't recall walking to the lake, and I definitely could not recall changing my clothes from a king's regalia to the black vest that I used to wear as prince. Despite the ominous vibes from the sharp wind and still water, my garments were rather comfortable. I'm sure there's a good analogy somewhere with cloth becoming more burdensome as life progresses, but I had no time for such thoughts. A man who could only be my father was knelt by the lake, staring intently into the waters. I searched for words but found none. Out of all the feelings that should have risen, apathy was the only one to make itself known.

"You still quiet, boy?" Father said, turning around to stare at me. The dead, purple skin on his neck was the final proof that I was, in fact, in a dream. He must have noticed me staring, as he said, "Surprised me too the first time I saw my reflection. Didn't think your mother had it in her. Gods, she was a gentle thing before you were born. You ruined my life, Orion. I hope you understand that."

Dream or not, what could I possibly say to such venom? I never asked to be born with Lepock's curse. I never asked for…well, anything really. In the end, all I wanted was Dorothy, but I somehow ended up with no Dorothy and an entire kingdom filled with people who despised me. "What kind of man blames his woes on a child? Anyway, you should be proud. I ended up being the heir you always wanted."

"Yeah, I've seen my so-called heir in action. Turning my home into a temple for the silent god."

"His name is Lepock." I smiled, and it was one of the few times I enjoyed not wearing a mask. I wanted him to see the smug look on my face. I wanted him to feel powerless in front of the son he never loved.

Instead, my father sighed and turned away, shaking his head. "I know his fucking name. He spoke to me in dreams before I tried to drown you. Warned me that success would lead to a lifetime and beyond of torment. I almost...I nearly decided against it."

It was odd to hear pain in his voice. Was this some sort of apology? I actually chuckled, then said, "But you did. What's the point of regret now? We're well past apologies. In fact, one of us is well past being alive—though I have a feeling that number may soon become two."

"Regret is a strange, yet terrible thing. At a certain point in a man's life, it evolves from a constant nagging to an overwhelming sense of dread. The worst is when we don't exactly know what to regret, yet still feel our heart yearning for a world that cannot exist thanks to our own failures. Orion, whatever you may think of me, I didn't...attempt to remove you from the realm out of hatred. I loved you with my entire heart, with every part of me. Loved you more than even your mother did. You were my *boy*. I just...couldn't allow you to be corrupted by that monster. Lepock. Fucking Lepock."

I really wished this dream would end. It was too much to take in at once. For reasons I still cannot explain, hearing my father's love was far more painful than holding his ire. It had been so easy to move on from a man who never loved me. Now...well, it really didn't matter. I had no one left to move on from. "I wish we could have had this conversation earlier," was all I could say. It wasn't a lie, more like a thought spoken out loud because there was nothing else to break the silence.

"Son…before this dream fades…please just…one time…tell me you loved me. So many burdens will leave my soul once I finally hear those words. I won't dare ask for forgiveness. I just want love. Please, just one last time, I just want love."

"I…I…I—"

The world went dark before I could respond. Hopefully, that meant the dream was over. I could still breathe, but each inhale/exhale made no sound. It had been quite a while since I'd had a nightmare. They had mostly ended since becoming king. Perhaps this was a side effect of Deaf's version of the Gift of Silence? Another reason to kill him. It would be tough on Coralie, but she would learn in time. If there was a hole in her heart, I would be happy to fill it with my love. Odd that I still hadn't woken up. Was I dead? I had always wondered what death was like. Maybe I could haunt people's dreams and yell philosophical ramblings at them—

Orion, my silent little king. You have squandered my gift, and more importantly: squandered my time. I can tolerate inaction no longer. Deaf has arrived, and with my chosen one comes a requiem of silence. I care not who prevails, as long as silence finally comes. I cannot rest…I need silence…I cannot rest…I need silence…I cannot rest…

The eye opened in the middle of the darkness. I could barely make out the wings but more importantly, I felt his power pressing against my body. It didn't seem like a dream. We're not supposed to feel pain in dreams. Not knowing if sound would come, I said, "Deaf desires nothing but chaos. Do you truly believe he will grant you rest?" I laughed at Lepock's naivety. Silent Almighty perhaps, but such a title makes it impossible to understand the complexity—and overall stupidity—of humans.

Let them laugh. Let them cry. I can accept their short-reigned cacophony as long as the end result is silence. Sometimes, the child must scream before falling into a deep slumber. Enjoy this taste of my reality. If madness follows, do not resist. It will all end eventually...

With or without you.

Before I could respond, Lepock faded from view. All was dark, all was quiet, until a barrage of screams hit me at once. I think I flinched, it was impossible to tell without sight. More like I shuddered, I shook, I tried to grab ears that were not there with hands that did not exist...

I heard everything. I have no idea how to describe it. Every little voice, every little scream, every little whisper. The shuffles of feet, the making of love, murders, thievery, drinks in a tavern. "Stop this. Please stop this," I said, or at least, I think I said. It was just another noise. Another voice upon the chorus of humanity—

I gasped awake, drenched in sweat. I immediately grabbed my mask to ensure it was still there. There was no longer a single person in the entire realm who had seen my true face and I intended for it to stay that way. To my surprise, Deaf's little sister was at my bedrest. I had given her the freedom to roam my castle—but not the freedom to leave.

"King Mute, did you have bad dream?"

I took a moment to lean forward and compose myself, and also made a mental note to keep my chamber door locked. If Deaf's sister was free to roam my castle, each sleep could be my last.

CHAPTER 5

MOTHER OF GOD

e are told that life is beautiful, though if that were the case, we wouldn't have to lie to our children. We tell them the lies they need to hear. Every word chosen with careful precision, navigating the gap between wisdom and trauma. But hard as we try, we never choose the right ones. Oh, the right words do come. They do. They must. Just years later, in the bath or in the pub. The ale burns our caution. And for a moment—a fleeting, terrible moment—we are prepared to tell them everything. Every little warning. Every little truth. But it's over. They have long left. We are alone, with all the knowledge in the realm and no one to pass it down to. Our former glory, amplified by each passing day. Our current shame, buried, faded, lost beneath a mask of pride.

"Hand me the sugar," I said to Coralie. Honestly, I just wanted to see if she would do it. Let me stop rambling and give some context. It was…uncomfortable since I had thrown Deaf into the dungeon. Coralie had never asked me to free him with words but she had constantly done so with her eyes. And let me tell you: they were *beautiful*. I probably would have said yes and let consequences fall where they lie.

"Hand King Mute the sugar, deary," Coralie said to her daughter—whose name I could not remember. Having the daughter here was the strangest aspect of Deaf's capture. Her constant stutters and shivers wounded my heart. Listen, I would never harm the girl. If we tried every child for the sins of their parents, the streets of Balewind would be covered in nooses.

Well, more so than they already were.

"No!" yelled the little girl, crossing her arms. "The king is stupid! He threw Noah in prison!"

"Norah!" Coraline yelled. I ignored the slight as it finally gave me the girl's name without asking. Hmm. Norah and Noah. It's difficult to trust parents who give their kids names with the same beginning letter.

"Now, now," I said with a smile, though no one could see it. "As an act of peace, the king shall fetch his own sugar." Since the sugar container—I really don't know what those things are called—was close, I grabbed it and added a dash to my tea. "Little Norah, what ails you this wonderful morning?"

Her eyes were watery. She kept looking at her mother before looking at me, probably terrified and having no idea what to do or what to say. Little did she know, it didn't matter. So many pawns think they are king until the knights arrive from the other side of the board. "I don't want Noah to die. You're going to kill my brother. I love him! I prayed to the Silent Almighty for you to spare him. I hope he answers my prayers…"

"Love is not a shield." In hindsight, they were not the best of words. When Norah started to whimper, I said, "Don't take that to heart. You have my oath, on whichever deity you favor, Noah will not be harmed." Again, I don't know why we lie to children. There is just something about their innocence. Even if it must end eventually, no man wants to be caught holding the dagger.

"Can I see him?" said Coralie. "This whole ordeal is a terrible misunderstanding. His actions were influenced by fear. The boy is fascinated by your relationship with the Silent Almighty. You are basically Deaf's hero."

Hero? Oh, for sure. Some lies are so desperate, all we can do is ignore them and wait for the liar to try again with a more dignified attempt. "Why does everyone call him that?"

"Deaf?" asked Coralie. "He wanted something…catchy. Something similar to the way you call yourself Mute."

"No, no. I understand that. It's the Silent Almighty that throws me off. I don't…I just…why?"

It was alarming how her eyes went wide. She put down her tea and said, "You saw his power." She paused and took a deep breath. After a rather uncomfortable silence, she said, "Because of Lepock, it was all worth it. Everything. All those years in the dens, all those years begging for scraps from worthless men. I have suffered wounds no woman should. But my boy…my boy is blessed. I knew from the moment I held him in my arms. Now, finally, I am the Mother of God."

My desire for this woman faded just a bit after hearing her nonsensical monologue. It's odd how no loves are created equal. My mother loved me as a protector. Saw me a thing that couldn't survive on its own, mere prey in a kingdom of predators. I don't really know how to describe Coralie's love. It was like…a justified hatred, manifested into a child-shaped weapon of silence.

"Pass the milk?" I said to Norah, who didn't seem interested in her mother's ramblings. She had probably heard it all before. Madness grows tiresome after a while when the message is simply, *"Look at me!"* or *"Hate this person or group!"*

"A shame that your mother passed," said Coralie. She seemed to have come to her senses—the weird look in her eyes reverted back to that effortless seduction. "From one mother to the next, I have so many questions. And thanks, all things considered. Keeping you alive is the reason I am here. She died never knowing who I was, and yet shaped the very fabric of my reality. Odd, how life works sometimes."

"Odd indeed," I said with a frown. No one ever passed me

the milk. Breakfast really wasn't going the way I had anticipated. Coralie was too damaged and complex to court her properly. Honestly, I missed women who wanted nothing more than gold. Now that, I could provide. "I have an idea. Finish your breakfast, then we'll visit little Noah."

Norah nearly fell from her chair in excitement. "Yay! Can I come too?"

"No."

***

We look at dungeons differently after attaining power. What was once a deterrent for crime and other dastardly behavior becomes a tool to control the masses. The noose isn't always the answer. Sometimes, the sharpest blade is to move a piece off the board and out of sight.

"Must it be so far down?" asked Coralie. "The dungeons in Ganfren are lateral instead of horizontal. Much more efficient."

It was tempting to ask how exactly she knew that but I moved on. Both with the conversation and my descent down the stairs. "I actually spent a few days there back in the days of King Lector Shaw. Ah, he was a kind soul. I miss the man."

She laughed. "That puts you in unique company. In my experience, whether out of fear or jealousy, everyone in power ends up hating each other—"

"Mother?" said a faint voice from the end of the halls. "Mother! Has this charlatan harmed you in any way? I'll ensure his torment lasts a lifetime. He will scream, and not a sound will be heard."

I really didn't like this guy. For someone named Deaf, it felt like all he ever did was speak. I smiled, then said, "I have a soft spot for mothers. She will never feel an ounce of pain. Physically, at least. As for you? Well, that depends heavily on your next words. Choose them carefully, Noah."

To his credit, Deaf did seem to hold his tongue. Perhaps he wanted a way out of this mess. Such a thing was possible, though very unlikely. "Have you passed judgment?"

I shrugged my shoulders. "Perhaps." Honestly, I just wanted to make him angry. Make him do one of those childish outbursts, giving me an excuse to hang him. After a day or two of mourning, I could invite his mother up to my chambers for an evening of tea and temptation.

"Your judgment cannot harm me," said Deaf. "The Silent Almighty spoke to me last night. He assured me that everything will be okay. All I must do is believe." Deaf rose and approached the bars. He tilted his head up and raised his arms high in the air. "Bestow upon me your pain, your illness, your sorrow. Silence will absolve them all. Though their tears will soil the earth, no man shall ever weep again."

"Deary," Coralie said, "if you beg for forgiveness, the king will allow you to remain alive through exile. We can return home! As I told you, we don't belong here. Balewind…Balewind is a terrible place, filled with terrible men."

"Precisely," said Deaf, before I could rebuke such nonsense. "Gods go where they are required. Trust me, Mother."

"I do." Coralie stepped back from the prison cell and wiped a tear from her eye. Strangely enough, despite being king, I felt invisible, and I was okay with that. It felt nice in a way. Most people don't wear a mask because they wish to be seen.

"Your Majesty," said Cyrus, who I hadn't even heard enter the dungeon. "Come to the throne room at once. There is an…emergency situation."

CHAPTER 6

SOLVING PROBLEMS BY FILLING GRAVES

 sat on my throne, tapping my fingers on the armrest. For an "emergency situation" so far it was people discussing various things in private, while their king sat and waited for words. "Well?" I finally said.

"Another cultist uprising," said Cyrus. "The incidents have increased since Deaf made his presence known. It's not easy for me to admit this, but I have failed you. Having the meeting take place in public was a tactical error. Shouldn't have taken place at all. Should have just hung them."

I leaned back and said, "Unfortunately, no one can hang the past." Things were truly dire if Cyrus was nervous. How many of these cultists were there? How did this happen under my leadership? "We'll need a plan, for starters. What are their numbers?"

"I don't know," my general said. "We should assume the worst. In all my days never could I imagine Lepock cultists spreading terror and confusion in the open. Oh, your father would have hung my entire family for such incompetence."

That felt like a slight, though I would let it go for now. To be fair, Cyrus was right. My father would've hung innocent and guilty alike without a moment's hesitation if it meant stability. I had always found such tactics cruel as a child. As an adult wearing a crown, I do admit there is merit to the "hang them all" method.

A few awkward moments passed. The silence from my general and advisors was a warning that I had surrounded myself with fools. I chuckled, then said, "Funny you should mention my father. Perhaps he was right all along. No need to overthink our scenario. Grab your armor. Grab your blades. Cultist is just another word for criminal. Let's put their faith to the test."

***

A few hours later, I stood outside my castle gates, surrounded by Cyrus and several armored soldiers: men, women, the young and old alike. I always favored equality when people were willing to die in my name. The pouring rain was fortunate as it would make the post-battle cleanup easier.

"Your Majesty," said Cyrus, "are you certain that you wish to join us? This sort of thing is…nasty business."

As an assassin who had murdered his way to the throne, I nearly laughed. It was wonderful to have such a man serve me. He knew who I was. I don't think he knew *why* I was, but to be fair: that one was still a mystery. "It's only violence, my friend. Nothing nasty about it as long as it's inflicted upon the enemy."

Cyrus offered a rare smile. "Fair enough. At least take my sword. I know you fancy daggers but in a real skirmish, you need to maintain distance."

The weapon my general offered was a fair one, but I waved it away. "Dagger will do just fine. After years of…'nasty business' I have become quite intimate with the blade. It's the little things we don't practice but learn in the field. Where to stab. Where *not* to stab."

"Very well, I know better than to question a king. But please, if nothing else: be safe." Cyrus patted me on the shoulder and approached the head of his unit. Was that…compassion? It was rare to receive any genuine concern, perhaps "Lord Deaf" would rethink his barbaric opinions of me if he could see how I inspired the commoners.

Well, not all commoners. Not the ones approaching from every direction. At least it spared us the effort of hunting them down. My hand shook as I reached for my dagger. I didn't want to die. Not because I enjoyed being alive, but none of these people deserved the honor of slaying the Silent King—the *true* Silent King. I didn't understand how or why there were so many. Sure, there had been reports of unrest, drugs, and cultists over the years, but I figured it would sort itself out in time. Well, perhaps "in time" had finally arrived. Solving problems by filling graves. Father would be proud.

Cyrus yelled, "Charge!" but it took a moment for my mind to comprehend the attack was beginning. Fortunately, two guards by my side remained close. They must have been assigned directly to me. Part of me welcomed the safety. The other part wished they would go away. I waited for everyone to engage before I made my move. I was never a loud walker—some are, you know the type— but I was practically silent as I drifted to a wounded cultist. Wounded men are the best targets. The odds of victory are most fortuitous when the enemy can't fight back. And, well, a kill is a kill. Anytime I had claimed to kill five or so men, no one had ever asked for details. Soldiers know better, and women simply don't care.

The man pointed at me before my dagger ripped open his throat. What a strange turn of events. Cultists worshiped Lepock, only to be slain by his chosen one. I don't know why they despised me. To be fair: I never asked. Hmm, the right flank of my unit was getting overrun. I felt sorry for my soldiers—many of them had enlisted to serve a king who had never learned their names, only to die at the hands of their own people.

I let the rain clean my blade as I approached the weakened flank. My two guards rushed in, and my adrenaline pumped as I realized I was finally alone. It was the closest thing to comfort I could find. Battlegrounds are always so *loud*. There was a solution to that.

I closed my eyes, cleared my mind, and focused on nothing. "Hush," I whispered, then the streets went deaf.

Ah, much better. The fighting continued, but my ears found relief from the noise. I analyzed the battleground, finding my personal guards from earlier butchered in the rain. They were loyal soldiers—whatever their names were. The four or so cultists who had slaughtered my men saw me and sprinted forward. I did not flee. First off: I wasn't fast enough to escape. But more importantly: I wanted them to come. If my people were losing faith in their king, I would give them something to believe in.

The first man found faith in the form of blood. It flowed out from his neck after I dodged his lazy strike and countered. People are too dependent on sound. They worship it like the sun or water, but really, it's nothing more than a hindrance. The next two were smart enough to attack in unison. I won't lie—a sword grazed my sides. I screamed, knowing full well nothing would happen. There were advantages to not having Deaf's gift. My shame would fade in silence, known only to myself and the eight or nine people who don't DNF this tale and demand a refund from Rainforest.

My counter swing missed. Without my gift, a loud whistle would've followed. Instead, I lost balance and fell on my side. A throbbing pain followed, and I immediately turned on my back to defend myself. I covered my neck and swung my dagger aimlessly like a drunken vagrant. I wept in the process. I don't care what you think of that.

It's a good time to mention that my father had been an incredible warrior. He rose to the rank of king the honorable way: fighting in battle after battle, gaining the loyalty of those with power, then using said power to remove the man who wielded a crown, fancy clothes, but no actual power.

Obviously, I didn't die this early in the story. That may or *may not* occur later. I never saw them, but by the time I stopped flailing my blade, I was surrounded by Cyrus and several guards. They watched me in various forms of disappointment, and it took a few seconds before Cyrus helped me rise. I believe a few of them were laughing. Bless the Gift of Silence for sparing me from such humiliation. My sides continued to throb as I stood and regained balance. Hmm. With the cultists slain, it didn't seem like their numbers had been so many. People always appear smaller from the ground. The Gift of Silence was a hindrance now that the danger was gone. I wanted to ask how, why, anything really, but all I could do was nod to my general and follow.

Rain is one of the few things less beautiful without sound. Without the gentle tapping on the rocky streets, it was like a dream manifested into reality. But even with the blur of water clouding my vision, I could watch my townsfolk recoil in horror as I headed back to the castle. What did these people want from me? I didn't bring the cultists here. Sure, we followed the same god, but they did it *wrong*. Listen, faith is the most wonderful, yet terrible thing I have ever experienced. It turns the humblest of men into servants of good deeds and charity, but also gives sadists an excuse to turn a clean blade red in the name of misconstrued words written hundreds of years ago.

I desired nothing more than a quick nap. By the time we reached the castle, my throbbing sides were burning. Absolutely burning. "What a day," I said out loud, startled at my own voice. It hadn't even been twenty minutes since the battle and sound had returned. Perhaps Deaf had been correct, in some regard. I was losing my touch. If Lepock had sent the boy as a test or a means to increase my power, I would welcome such a challenge. I would enter my castle, shake the boy's hand, and demand peace. With his mother by my side and eventually in my bed, I could teach the boy what it meant to be king.

A guard rushed up to Cyrus. After some words I couldn't hear, Cyrus sighed. He approached me, then said, "Your Majesty, I bear unfortunate news. Cultist insurgents broke into the castle. Lord Deaf has escaped."

CHAPTER 7

Silent Charlatans

Unfortunately, nap time would have to wait. All sorts of guards and visitors were scurrying around the throne room, yelling to each other, to themselves, to anyone who cared to listen. How I wish I could call upon my gift once more. Damn those cultists. What a terrible way to draw attention from my grand victory. Oh, that had probably been the point. Diversion.

"King Mute," Coralie said, to my surprise. "We must speak at once."

I had no idea how to respond. Why hadn't she fled with her son? "Apprehend her!" I yelled. When no one responded I yelled, "Apprehend her. Now!" One of the few disadvantages to wearing a mask was how I couldn't wipe the sweat off my face. What a miserable day. Aside from my ribs, my entire head throbbed. I was just so tired. So very, very tired.

"To the dungeons?" asked Cyrus.

I scoffed. "Don't bother. The dungeons are obviously compromised. Maybe you can help me understand how someone, anyone, snuck a man from the lowest floor all the way out of the castle? I need answers. Or at the very least, leads. Something. Give me anything." I didn't mean to sound desperate. I forget where I read it but, desperation is certainly not a virtue.

After an awkward silence, Cyrus said, "All in time, Your Majesty. My investigation will take some work but…early intuition suspects a rat."

"A what?"

"Someone on the inside. Does anyone in your ranks hold fanatical beliefs for the so-called Silent Almighty?"

"Fanatical beliefs…" I groaned and rubbed the side of my head. It really wasn't the day for riddles. Most of the people by my side were too stupid and lazy to betray me. Cyrus was the only one with the mind for such treachery, but I trusted the man. I really did.

At the time, I believed he was a friend.

"What about you?" I asked Coralie. "What are you even doing here? Says much about your 'Lord Deaf' that he would abandon you to my judgment. I would never abandon my own mother. *Never.*" As I'm sure my brother would love to point out, I had done terrible things in my life. But listen, I never betrayed Mother. She had gone to her grave loving me, probably aware she would be the only one.

"I care not what my punishment is," said Coralie. "But give your word that Norah will not be harmed. She is innocent from this game of silent charlatans."

"You don't deserve my word." I glared at her—which was silly in hindsight considering she couldn't see it. Or perhaps she could. A child's mask is always invisible in the eyes of a mother. "Be grateful I don't harm children. They are innocent of their parent's sins, but there is a line. Pray you never find it." Yes, I know, the words were weak. I just didn't know what else to say. Murdering the little girl wouldn't fix my problems. I suspect it *would* have made my people cheer, which is an incredibly sad commentary on my reign thus far. Coralie responded but I turned away and never heard it. In hindsight, I wish I knew what she had said. Oh, how I wish I knew…

"Your Majesty," said Cyrus. "Pardon my intrusion but your wounds are showing. It would be ideal to rest up and let me investigate. If you fall, all is lost."

The genuine concern in his voice warmed my heart. "The day may indeed come, friend. In the case of my demise, don't follow me to the grave. I'm not going to heaven. I don't exactly know where my story ends, but I imagine there will be fire."

"Not fire, Your Majesty. Not anything at all. Only silence."

That statement was kind of weird. I didn't know how to respond, so I nodded and left towards the stairs to my chambers. Ugh, it was a long way up. Each step aggravated my ribs and, for whatever reason, other various aches all around my body. I don't know why everything hurt. The blade had only grazed my sides. Not sure how that translated to an injured foot.

Sorry, climbing stairs isn't very interesting. Let's move forward a bit to where I'm lying in bed with most of my clothes off after a healer had patched me up. My breathing slowed as I leaned my head into the pillow. I closed my eyes for a few moments but nothing happened. There was too much on my mind: Deaf, Coralie, Norah, General…Dorothy. Ah, it always went back to Dorothy. If she had just been a good woman and married me, I wouldn't be in this mess. Who knows, maybe I would be laughing in the town square, holding a little girl in my arms with Dorothy by my side. That would have been a nice life. Instead, I was King Mute, herald of the Silent God, hated by all of his followers. I held my mask with both hands and analyzed it. It was like staring into my own face.

Did the common folk dream of being king? Did they dream of being *me*? I could only wonder. I wish they could observe moments like this. Maybe that's why I wrote my tale in the first place. I am not a monster. Yes, of course, every monster says that. But…I'm not. Whatever you may believe, I'm not a monster.

I just wanted to be happy.

***

I hadn't slept well last night, but staring into my mask had given me the grandest of ideas. A revelation of sorts. If my mask was indeed my face, then my face could become a mask.

"Good evening, Your Majesty," said Cyrus with a bow. "You look well, all things considered. What brings you to the throne room? You need rest! Next time, send a servant my way and I can come to your chambers."

I leaned forward and said, "This request is for your ears only. I require clothes. Commoner's clothes. The full regalia. Boots, shirts, pants. Whatever those people wear."

My general's eyes went wide. "What trickery is this? You're not fleeing, are you? Don't do that to me. Don't you *dare* do that to me after everything."

Flee? Strangely enough, I had never even considered fleeing until that moment. It wasn't a terrible idea. Maybe I could hop on a boat and just…start over. What a content way to end the story. But then I would never see Dorothy again. No, I would follow my path, in dedication to my mom and brother. Their deaths would not be in vain.

"Not flee," I said, which I still don't know if that was a lie. "But infiltrate. I want to understand these people. What drives them, how their day-to-day goes, what inspires a man to worship a god that despises them. Surely you understand."

"I wish I did. A word of advice, if it pleases you?"

I hate that question because the only acceptable answer is, "Of course."

"Intelligence is a dangerous game. Leave recon to the expendable. If there is any constant trait among people from all walks of life, it's that they guard knowledge with their lives. Your idea is not without merit but, unfortunately, it is not without risk."

I sighed. "To save time, can I just command you to retrieve clothes?"

"Mute…Your Majesty…Very well. If nothing else, at least take your dagger."

"If it makes you feel better, then sure, but my skills have declined as my years have increased. You saw me out there yesterday. A rather unfortunate showing for a king." I snickered, and waited for his own laughter. Friends always laugh at their friend's unfunny jokes. That's how things are supposed to work.

Instead, Cyrus gently tapped me on the neck. "If you get caught, the dagger is not for them. These are terrible people, my lord. If you believe that we hide the horrors of war from the bard songs, you would not even *imagine* the things I keep from you." He left, presumably to retrieve my clothes.

In hindsight, I should have taken his advice. Nothing but terrible things awaited me in the den of silence.

CHAPTER 8

FLOODGATES TO ABSURDITY

ow do I look?" I asked Cyrus, while I stared into the mirror. It was…surreal to gaze upon myself. It was a disguise of course, but it was me. As you may have guessed, my face was very pale. Hiding from the sun all those decades had taken an exceptionally white toll.

"When you enter enemy territory, try not to speak. I don't see you, but your voice is distinct. A tad ironic for the silent king."

I smiled, before realizing he could see it. I didn't have the face for smiles or laughter. Some people are born with beauty. Others are born to hate the beautiful. Perhaps I could blame the clothes. Wrinkly white shirt, brown trousers, and I swear the shoes were red. What sort of man wears red shoes? I sighed and turned away, pulling up my socks after a few steps. It's funny how no one ever teaches us how there are different qualities of cloth. I always assumed sheep were thrown into the "wool apparatus" then turned into coats or however that worked. "I hardly recognize myself. I suppose that's a good thing."

"Indeed! I feel the same when my armor comes off. Very well, if I cannot convince you to abandon this mad task, then I shall do my part in ensuring that everything goes to plan. Your chamber doors will remain closed. Word will be spread that you are recovering from your heroic antics of vanquishing the cultists. I am holding a dinner in your honor. Not my finest hour, but true servants always find a way. Ah, Mute. Sometimes I wish you had a queen."

"As do I, friend, but women aren't exactly lining up for the opportunity." I tugged my shirt a final time and casually left my chambers. It was difficult to choose a correct walk. Less authority than a king. Less sneaky than an assassin. The goal was to walk normally, but that was even worse. Apparently, there is nothing less natural than trying to imitate normal. I eventually settled on a "strut" of sorts. I don't really know how to describe it. It was like the confident walk of a man who had secured an evening with a lady without having to pay her gold—

I nearly fainted when I entered the throne room. There was indeed a feast, with a golden table in the middle of the room, soldiers and noblemen chatting and slamming drinks. No one looked at me. And why would they? I was a shadow within a room of shadows. A commoner who had stumbled into a feast far above his station. I kept my head down and shuffled out of the room. At least I found my walk. It was the walk I did anytime Father had scolded or beaten me. Shame may fade for a time but never leaves completely. It lingers, waiting for us to be happy, then reminding us why we should never entertain such nonsense.

No one stopped me or paid any notice as I exited the castle. I couldn't blame them, for such is the rule of luxury: poverty is free to leave but poverty must not enter. My nerves calmed as I stepped into the marketplace. There was nothing to fear. Nothing to dread. I was nothing. *Nothing!* And it was beautiful. Wonderful. Perfect in every sense of the word.

But I had a job to do and, to be honest, I had no idea how to achieve my task. Could I simply walk up to people and request information? I should've bought something to prove I was king in case things went south, but I had brought nothing. It was exciting, in a way. Success or death. Either option seemed favorable.

"Offer your silent repentance!" a man yelled in the middle of the marketplace. "The Silent Almighty offers salvation! All you must do is hush."

I didn't mean to stare. I was just so taken aback to see people recruiting cultists in the open. Funny enough, this had been my doing. In legalizing Lepock's name, I had opened the floodgates to absurdity. And to think my nemesis believed I had done *too little* to spread silent influence? I just couldn't win with these people.

"You there!" the man said, pointing at me, to my utmost shock. "Come forth! Offer repentance! Accept the warm divinity from the Silent Almighty!"

I didn't mean to freeze. I thought he recognized me. I thought that at any moment, swords and screams would descend upon me from all directions, sending the Silent King to a silent grave. Instead, the man kept yelling. He wasn't very motivating, but he was loud. Sometimes, that's all it takes. "I…I could find repentance?"

"Of course! You shall speak your sins in the presence of the Silent Almighty, then you shall never speak again. I assure you, tis a silent, wonderful thing." It was odd how the man preaching silence wouldn't stop speaking.

After a bow I said, "Thank you for this grand opportunity, my lord. How do I sign up?"

I did not expect him to grab me. One of the several disadvantages of my oversized shirt was giving him a powerful grip. It made me miss the leather from my assassin days. Tight leather wasn't simply to impress the ladies. The cultist pulled me close and said, "Choose carefully, brother. Faith is a one-way road. Don't begin this journey unless you are prepared to join us in mind and spirit. There are no heretics, if you catch my drift."

One way road? For such an overused cliche, the phrase never made sense to me. Life itself is a one-way road. No matter how we spend the middle, that final chapter is always darkness. I would have to be convincing. While theater had never been my strong point, decades of lying to myself had made me quite proficient at deception. "My choice was made long before I met you. Question my faith again at your own risk."

Fortunately, my threat only made him smile. "Well said, brother. We need more men with anger and passion. I have one last question before we proceed. What is your opinion on the so-called king?"

I appreciated how he added "so-called" at the end to guide me to the correct answer. This time, fortunately, there was no need to lie. "I despise Mute more than any man alive."

"You do, don't you? Very well. Such timing is fortuitous. The next congregation begins at sundown."

"Wonderful. Lead the way…my lord." I had to remind myself to call him "my lord" at every opportunity. Hopefully that was his rank. It's always difficult with fanatics.

"Julian will suffice, brother. You'll learn to unlearn all the absurd ranks and constructs of royalty. Want to hear a secret? It's all made up. There are no lords, ladies, kings, any of that. There is only the Silent Almighty. Nothing else matters."

Against my better judgment, I asked, "What of Lord Deaf? Is he not the leader? When I heard rumors of escape, I…cannot describe the euphoria which overcame me. Lord Deaf is, well, he is the one…who made me believe."

"Correct. While everyone is equal, Lord Deaf is a step above brotherhood, second only to the Silent Almighty himself." I was beginning to suspect that like most cults, they were making up the rules as they went along. I had so many more questions: who funded this thing? Who supplied the black robes?

I took a deep breath. It was time. "Will you show me the way?"

"Indeed I shall. Come forth, brother. Lord Deaf awaits."

***

The journey to the run-down cathedral was a pitiful one. We had traveled the dusty roads of the slums, where various men, women, and even children begged me for gold. For the first time in my life, I truly had nothing to offer. Dust addicts were passed out in the middle of the streets. One man had apparently taken too much before his breathing stopped. Instead of rushing to his aid, vagrants rushed to his pockets. I think he died. To this day, I still don't know. To this day, I still don't care. I had ensured not to comment on such depravity. My guide would assume this was all commonplace for someone of my station. It's difficult to dream of crowns when all you desire is a night of safety and warm soup.

"Here we are, brother," Julian said. "Wait here, I'll grab you a pair of robes."

How tragic, I had spent all that time wondering about my wardrobe only to get a new one. When Julian returned, he handed me a black robe. It was a perfect fit. I was *very* tempted to ask how he knew my size but I figured he had experience with recruiting the desperate.

"Will I meet him? Lord Deaf, I mean."

"Oh, of course. He always takes time to meet recruits. A quick warning: I know you mentioned your dislike for Mute. Personally, I have my doubts. I've seen Deaf make an example out of false believers. Don't let that be you."

I laughed out loud, ignoring the fact that he could see my face. "I have been accused of terrible lies, brother, but I assure you, my loathing for Mute is genuine. I shall speak on this subject no more. Either take me at my word, or take me to my grave."

My self-loathing must have carried into my voice. He guided me inside without a sound.

CHAPTER 9

SILENCE WILL ABSOLVE THEM ALL

he first thing I noticed was a lack of sound. No, it wasn't completely silent: torches crackled in the corners of the cathedral, illuminating some—but not all—of the holy grounds. Some coughs and shuffles of feet, but for a room with at least one hundred or so robed followers, it was quieter than my father's funeral.

Sorry, I usually skip descriptions to move things along, but they are necessary here. You need to understand how beautiful it was. You need to understand how it wounded me. For the first time since I had become king, I wondered if I had been wrong. About love, about life, about…everything. What had I done for the past thirty-six years? How had I not learned to be happy? Even the destitute wallowing in their own filth laughed in the streets of Balewind. Was I no better than them? Was I *worse*?

"It's wonderful," I whispered. While I hoped it would be near-silent, the reverb of the cathedral made my error bounce at myself, over and over.

My guide didn't respond. He simply smiled and made a hush motion with his finger. Oh, the irony of it all. I followed him through the crowds to where, I did not know. The lack of sound made my eyes bold. I glanced at my brothers and assumed the women were sisters, though I never followed up on that. A few of them stared back. I didn't mean for our eyes to meet, but I was so used to wearing a mask that it took a few moments to turn away. No need for attention. The quickest way to draw unwanted attention is to be annoying.

I stopped moving when Julian did. We apparently had found our spot among the crowd. I will admit, my nerves made each breath louder than necessary. It was too cramped. For a giant hall, I had no idea why they only utilized half the room. A terrible way to spread illness, though I doubt anyone here was meant for a long life, myself included. The torches in the back went out, leaving the remaining two to illuminate what appeared to be an altar in front of us—a trick I was familiar with. Higher grounds are a means to show power.

"Brace yourself, brother," Julian whispered.

Okay, I'll admit, a touch of excitement from the anticipation made my heart race. It was like being in a theater show, except one of the actors may end up stabbing me. And there he was: Lord Deaf in all his glory. Upon his altar, he appeared much taller than when I had thrown him in prison. I held back a shiver from his mask. It would never feel normal to stare into the face of Lepock, though I admired it in a way. Deaf had taken a nightmare, a vision that would have driven the mightiest of soldiers to gibbering madness, and shaped it into his identity. There was no terror. There was no fear.

And if there was, no one would ever see it.

"Rejoice, brothers," Deaf yelled. Like most tyrannical laws, his silence was a rule meant to be followed by everyone other than himself. "For I have returned. I have returned from a journey. I have returned from a pilgrimage." It took a fair amount of constraint not to sigh. Listen, not all of us are good speakers. It's a gift I'll never wield, but it's important to come to terms with such limitations and spare everyone else.

"I entered the very den of heresy itself. A den of corruption and sin. A den manipulated by a false king. Care to guess what I found, brothers? A coward. A man unworthy to wield the gift of the Silent Almighty. Mute's time shall come. The final pillar between our people and prosperity is the heretic wielding a crown." Deaf approached the middle of the altar. After a few moments of silence, he raised his arms into the air, then said, "Bestow upon me your pain, your illness, your sorrow. Silence will absolve them all. Though their tears will soil the earth, no man shall ever weep again. Amen."

I nearly jumped when all of the followers responded, "Amen" in unison. Wasn't silence the whole point of this brotherhood? Perhaps not. I had a sneaking suspicion it was all a ploy to hoist a dangerous man upon the throne. A *more* dangerous man, to be fair.

Deaf came down from his altar and greeted the people in the front row. While he spoke and gave random words of encouragement, none of them spoke back. They bowed, knelt, one even whimpered as he wiped a tear from his eye. Hmm, at his current rate, it would take a while before he reached me. I wasn't all the way in the back, but more in the middle: a purgatory, of sorts.

"Whatever you do," Julian whispered, "don't speak. Even to answer a question. Just keep your eyes low and your mouth closed. I've lost some good recruits to bad decisions here. I get a vial of dust for each one of you people that joins the cause. Don't ruin this for me."

Odd that he felt the need to tell me that. Now that he mentioned it, his hands were a little shaky and his eyes bloodshot. In hindsight, the rise of dust and heretics was less of a coincidence than Cyrus had suggested. Assuming I escaped from here, there was much to ponder.

I cannot recall how long it took for Deaf to reach me. My most prominent thought at the time was, why weren't there any chairs? But eventually, the wooden mask of Lepock himself reached my row. He shook hands, gave blessings, never receiving a word or a sound in return. I took a deep breath as he approached the man next to me. I watched every gesture, heard every word, but couldn't tell you a thing that happened. My mind was too busy injecting me with anxiety. Deaf would recognize my face. He would recognize my body. Perhaps he could feel the power of Lepock inside me. I couldn't do that but, then again, I hadn't mastered my powers to Deaf's level. I had squandered my years sitting on a throne doing nothing, approving every notion, ignoring every threat, in order to make the day end faster…

"Welcome, brother," said Deaf. I'm not afraid to admit that I flinched. "Tis rare to see a man of your age join the cause." Deaf analyzed me like I was a horse, rubbing his chin and not making a sound. He eventually said, "You have an aura about you. There is blood on your hands. Tell me, and speak true: are you a rapist, or a murderer?"

"I am no rapist." I know, I wasn't supposed to speak, but some accusations must be refuted. I had done terrible things. Ruined many lives. But never, and I mean *never*, had I crossed such a line. Like any true gentleman, I always ensured my lovers were paid.

A few gasps filled the air. They were startling, but anxiety made my eyes twitch after Julian backed away. "Murderer then," said Deaf. "No shame in that, brother. My hands are stained red and shall never know purity again. Tis the price of action. Words only get us through the door. To change the world, more…let's call it effort, is required."

"Murderer and hero are one of the same cloth. It just depends on which side prevails. I wield no regrets, Lord Deaf." Sadly, none of those words were lies. Regret is such a foolish notion. The past is invincible. I have seen gods, monsters, all sorts of things in all their glory. I have never seen yesterday crumble.

"Side?" Lord deaf chuckled. He glanced around the room, provoking most of them to chuckle back. "This is not a war. This is a revolution. The only side is the one still remaining after the rain falls."

"Rain is a volatile thing. In my most sorrowful moments, I swear the clouds last forever."

Lord Deaf placed a hand on my shoulder. I think it was to comfort me. To this day, I still don't know. "You see the world with your ears and listen only with your eyes. Give me your faith, brother. I swear I will make sense of it all."

The sad thing was, I believed him. Not that he was telling the truth, but that he believed every word. Was I ever so naive? Delusional, perhaps, though I like to think I improved in my older years. I'll have to wait and see how the wonderful people on Pleasant Reads judge me after this tale. Out of words, all I could do was bow. I kept my eyes closed in case he stabbed me. I had no desire to witness my own end. Judge me as craven if you must, but I wager you would do the same in my position.

But nothing happened. It's impossible to say how many seconds or minutes passed but, eventually, Deaf said, "You are a mystery that I wish to unravel. Join me in my chambers after the congregation." He didn't wait for a response. Deaf simply nodded at Julian, then proceeded to greet the next recruit. Unlike me, none of them spoke.

After the congregation ended, I watched the robed followers scurry away in various directions. It was tempting to follow them, to find out who they were and where they were going, but Julian grabbed me and pulled me close. "You dumb son of a bitch. I don't know whether to hug or strangle you. Be careful in there. You are my recruit. Whatever you do or say reflects directly on me. Don't fuck this up. I need my dust. Do you understand me? *I need my dust.*" I wished he would let me go. The "dust people" or whatever you wish to call them were all mad. I had sent so many of them to the noose, it would be fitting if one of their kind did me in. Julian must have come to his senses. He patted me on the shoulder and walked away, his eyes lost and nearly glazed over.

This left me in an odd position. I didn't know where Deaf's chambers were. Fortunately, a robed man whispered in my ear, "Come. You are expected."

CHAPTER 10

SILENT MONSTERS

n hindsight, it was no surprise that Deaf's chambers were behind the altar. It felt wrong to walk across, and even worse as I passed the statue of Lepock. I swear the eye followed my every movement. I admired the detail of the statue before my guide gave me a not-so-gentle push towards a wooden door.

No words were spoken, but I assumed that was my cue to enter. I opened the door. It felt like entering Eleanor's brothel, but the only thing awaiting me inside was Lord Deaf and…

It was her. I could hardly believe it. Perhaps I had died and gone to heaven. Or perhaps I had died and gone to a prison of fire, burning away the few things that still brought joy. "Dorothy?" I said. The question was one word but may as well have been an epitaph. Like most priceless treasures, I had found her by searching for something less beautiful. I no longer cared about Deaf. I no longer cared about Coralie. I no longer cared about the daughter, whose name I had forgotten several chapters ago.

It was her. It was Dorothy. Her skin had aged like a fine wine. The circles under her eyes told the story of a woman yearning for her king. She was slender, her hands shook, she was…

She was perfect. If you gain nothing else from this story, I want you to understand that. I *need* you to understand that.

"So it is you," said Deaf. He chuckled then, to my surprise, removed his mask. Similar to my own, his face was pale and tired. Apparently, there are several disadvantages to ignoring the sun. "I'll never understand what you see in this woman. So common. So plain. You are a weak man, Orion. The throne does not suit you. The Silent Almighty does not suit you."

"You will never hear your own voice again." Every part of my body shook after I spoke. I was so confused with rage that I couldn't force out any other words. There was so much to say, so much to yell. If this "Lord Deaf" had harmed Dorothy in any way, his house of worship would become a house of graves. As I'm sure you have concluded by now, I am not a good man. I would kill them all without hesitation. And my conscience would rest easy, as it always did.

Deaf gestured to the open spot across the table. "Never threaten a god within his own domain. Trust me, if I wished you dead, such an outcome would already have come to pass. Besides, you should thank me. To my knowledge, you have been pursuing this woman for years. I found her almost immediately."

"Oh Dorothy," I said, taking my seat. Rage would do me no good. I would slay Deaf eventually, but there were greater matters at hand. "Where have you been? Why did you abandon me?"

She glared at me. I swear it was so spiteful, I nearly wept. I would have traded my entire kingdom and all of my wealth for a simple mask. Emotions are never meant to be seen. We keep them inside, only for our face to betray our true feelings. "I care not what happens to me. My son is safe within the kingdom of Ganfren. I am content to act the pawn in this game of silent monsters."

"Dorothy…I…just tell me: where have you been? I searched everywhere. Every brothel, every inn, every gambling den. I had assumed the worst. I thought you left our realm. This…to see you now…there are no words to adequately—"

Deaf chuckled. "She was always here, residing in the kingdom of Balewind. Such is the limitation of eyes, brother. In attempting to see everything, we see nothing at all."

"There is nothing stopping me from slaying you in this chamber." I thanked each one of the vile gods that my voice did not crack. I knew the words were weak, but they were all I had left. That, and my dagger. I took off my robe and put my hand on the hilt.

"There are several things," said Deaf, still not rising from his seat. "Most importantly, all of your violence was done within the safety of shadows. Such tactics are irrelevant in my domain. I control the whispers. I control the darkness. Violence only occurs when I am the one wielding the blade." He again gestured to my seat. Against all the rage and bravado coursing through my blood, I sat.

"I met your conditions," said Dorothy. Her shaky hands could barely hold her chalice of wine. "Please give me the dust and allow my return to Ganfren. There is nothing for me here. Every corner of every road, every bakery, every inn…the memories are all nightmares."

I sighed. "It didn't have to be this way. I would have given you everything. The boy too, whatever his name is. You would have been Queen Dorothy, beloved ruler of Balewind."

Deaf rose with a chalice in his hand. He took a few steps away from the table and turned his back to me. "Lepock still favors you. I do not know why, but to question the Silent Almighty is not my prerogative. So I offer you a choice. A courtesy between brothers, if you will. There are many roads ahead of us, but none end with you remaining as king. Listen, I hold no love for you. In my eyes, you are an incompetent fool, floundering the glory of God with no understanding how or why the realm operates…"

"Is there a proposal or are you going to stand there and berate me? You could at least offer some wine."

"I suppose I could," said Deaf. He walked back to the table and filled a chalice. To my relief, the wine bottle was already open and nearly empty. While it didn't completely negate the possibility of poison, it lowered the odds enough to where I didn't care. To be honest, poison didn't sound all that bad after seeing Dorothy in her current state. "My proposal is as follows: take Dorothy and vanish. Head back to Ganfren if you prefer. I care not, as long as you no longer reside here. And I chose the word vanish carefully. No death, no war, no violence. Most importantly: no martyrs. Faith is a very fragile thing, brother. There is something about dead fools that drives the living to fight in their honor—"

"*No!*" yelled Dorothy. And when I say yelled, I mean it nearly resembled a scream. The screech hurt my ears but more importantly, my heart. She wanted nothing to do with me. Even after all these years. Looking back, I do not believe time heals all wounds. In fact, I believe time does nothing but carry on.

But…

But, I had to try. Right? That had been the whole point of this journey. I had searched for enlightenment and instead found heaven. I decided to be bold. My hand eased across the table to Dorothy's. She immediately smacked my hand away and nearly jumped out of her seat. Her eyes darted towards the exit. I am not ashamed to say I rose and blocked her path. No, stop, it wasn't like that. I just didn't want her to leave. It was dangerous outside! She needed protection. She needed warmth. She needed…

Well, she needed me.

"*Let go of me!*" she screamed, pounding both fists into my chest. "Monster! You were always a monster! Why can't I ever escape? The nightmare never ends."

Nightmare? After all that time, after all those years, I was just a nightmare? Rather unfair. I had experienced several nightmares after becoming king. For all their horrors, none of them ever resembled my tired face. I eased my grip, hoping she wouldn't immediately run off. "Even now, is that all I am to you? Why could you never love me?"

"I don't know, Mute. I never…feelings are never a choice. Listen, I apologize for calling you a monster, but you will never wield my heart. If there is any part of you that holds feelings beyond your base desires then…please let me go. Don't follow me to Ganfren. Our journeys are no longer intertwined. The story is over."

I knew the words were true. Maybe one day, I would look back on this exchange and appreciate the closure. At the time, I didn't feel anything. Apathy was a familiar state of mind. The numbness, the cold embrace of knowing nothing really mattered. I let her go. Both in the physical sense, and the part of my heart that yearned for a different reality. Unfortunately, yearning for things doesn't make them happen. The moment was lost. I was lost. Strangely enough, the epiphany made me invincible. Deaf could not harm me. I mean, yes, he could quite easily harm my body, but my heart was already dead.

"I love you," I whispered. "I will treasure you forever, but I will never bother you again. You are free of me. Go forth and find the happiness I could never provide."

Dorothy whispered back. No, I won't repeat the words. They were for my ears only. They were not poetic, they were not beautiful. I…I don't really know how to describe them. They were words spoken to someone she never loved. The rest doesn't matter. Use your imagination if you must. She ran off, and I did not watch. I instead drank my entire chalice, letting the faint burn take its toll before the numbness would caress me.

"You are a strange man," Deaf said, stepping closer to the table. "What do you desire? I thought I had you figured out."

I couldn't help but laugh. "Sorry, Brother. After all these

years, I still have no idea. Seems like a fine day to die. Am I free to leave or shall we dance with daggers?"

Deaf finished his chalice and placed it on the table. "What else could you possibly desire?" he whispered. After a few moments he yelled, "*What do you want?* I have tried to be merciful. Are you a test from the Silent Almighty? There is no other possibility." He drew a dagger from his side. "Very well. God will forgive me in time. Make peace with your sins, Orion. In a moment you shall—"

"Norah is still in my possession. Would be unfortunate if news of my demise reached the castle." It was a good time to remember her name. I don't blame you for believing me to be craven. Tis a fair accusation. For whatever reason, I yearned to persevere. Despite losing my kingdom. Despite losing my god. Despite losing Dorothy. The realm would be better off with my demise, but still, there was no reason to rush such things.

Deaf scoffed. If he meant it as a dismissive gesture, I saw right through his bluff. There was fear in his eyes at the mention of Norah. I never had a sister. It's…nearly impossible to imagine loving my brother to such an extent. "You wouldn't harm her. Not out of honor or pride, but cowardice. I can see right through you."

Feeling bold, I stepped forward, meeting him face-to-face. What a strange sight. Two below-average looking men with daggers in their hands. Two men who in better days, perhaps, could have been friends. "The only woman I ever loved just called me a monster and fled. Balewind rots as my people inject dust and murder each other in the streets. I preside over a kingdom of empty bellies and full nooses. I dare you to wager upon my compassion."

His hesitation told me everything. Silence was one of the few things I truly understood. The moment was a rush of clarity. I was better than this man. I knew it. Lepock knew it. Deep down, perhaps Deaf had come to the same conclusion. "Get out of my sight," he said, turning away. "You have five days to return my family. After said timeframe, I shall consider them lost. Mute, if such a thing occurs, the comfort of silence will never caress you again. Every morning will be filled with the screams I tear from your body. Martyr? No. You will be a warning never to blaspheme against the Silent Almighty. You have five days, *Your Majesty*. Cherish them."

"Five won't be necessary. Come to my castle tomorrow evening. You shall have them both. Oh, and bring your dagger. It's about time we settled this. Two kings is always one too many."

"You take me for a fool?"

"My feelings are irrelevant in the matter. Pray to Lepock and think about it. You're a bright lad. In the end, you'll make the right choice." Then, I simply walked away. Whether delusion or arrogance, I had no fear that he would retaliate. I had given him every madman's dream: a legitimate path to power. All he had to do was take it. All he had to do was murder the silent king.

I walked past the altar and down the stairs, towards the exit from this nightmare. I nearly jumped when Julian grabbed me. For such a bag of woe and depravity, the man moved with a silence that would put Lepock to shame.

"Brother!" he yelled. "You live! Oh, I'll admit, I was a worried man. Wouldn't want anything to happen to my special friend. More dust. More dust will come my way. What a beautiful day to live, brother!"

I doubt Julian expected me to pull him in close and embrace him with all my strength. "Forgive me, for I have failed you. I have failed you all. I may not hear you, brother, but I see you. And I will never lose sight of you again." I kissed Julian on the forehead and stepped away. Listen, I'm willing to admit that I had been a terrible king. It was never by choice. These things just sort of…happen. I'm not here to claim I would do better.

Simply speaking, I was prepared to die.

CHAPTER II

ARCHITECT OF WOE

he rain was more frustrating without a mask. I felt each drop upon my face, squinting my eyes to ensure I didn't stumble into any of the dust-addicted vagrants in my path. There were many—oh, so many. Cyrus had said this problem had been "mostly resolved." Perhaps we had a different definition of either word.

By instinct, I met eyes with all sorts of villagers and vermin, and forgot to look away. It would be nice to wear my mask again. To avoid the horrors of personal interactions. In my journey to the castle, I passed no-less than ten cultist recruiters. They were *everywhere*. It was all becoming clear. Whether to protect my pride or some other sinister reason, Cyrus had been lying to me. A moment of panic came when I reached the castle gates. I had brought no evidence of my identity. It seemed unlikely I could silver-tongue my way back to the throne.

"State your business!" the guard said, pointing his halberd at me. A bit unnecessary, but I couldn't blame the man. By nature, dealing with filth all day will make any man less gentleman-like. "There is no bread for you here! Be gone, vagrant!"

"Bread?" I could hardly contain my laughter. It wasn't until now that I realized I was starving. Sorry, I know that veers a bit close to the "letting out a breath I didn't know I was holding" territory, but I swear it all hit me at once. "I did not come here for bread. Escort me to the throne room, or fetch General Cyrus."

"Cyrus? How dare you invoke his name!" the guard continued his outraged yells, and all I could do was sigh. To be fair, I had been working this all wrong. It wasn't a silver tongue I required, but quite the opposite.

"Hush," I whispered, then the castle gates and everything around us went deaf.

All the rage left the guard's face, replaced by what I assumed was terror. For however much I yearned to find love, at least I could always fall back on fear. He opened the gates immediately, moved out of my path and knelt. More guards flowed out from the castle as I made my approach.

I tried to say, "Thank you" as I passed them, just to see if it would work. It did not. Oh well, I didn't see the practicality for such an ability, anyway.

I covered my face as Cyrus rushed out of the castle with dinner guests behind him. He would know it was me, and that discretion was necessary. Fortunately, none of them paid me any mind. And why would they? I looked poor and desperate. Such a combination was worthless in the eyes of the elite.

My general was kind enough to mouth, *Are you well, Your Majesty?* I couldn't tell if it was genuine without sound, though, to be honest, I probably couldn't tell anyway.

Yes, I mouthed back. It was a lie, but it's not like it mattered. I had several problems, several woes, but one of them could be fixed immediately. I slowly walked through my castle. Stress and fatigue were hitting harder now that my bed was within reach. It was easy to ignore the silent chaos. One would expect my people would be used to such a thing by now. After far too many stairs, my bed was there to welcome me. The silky sheets were soft and glorious. With Dorothy gone, it was the closest thing to heaven I would ever know.

***

Part of me was surprised to wake. I coughed, which meant my rest had been long enough for sound to return. Ah, my mask lay on my dresser. It stared at me, judging me, wondering why I had fled after all those years. No need to worry, old friend. I placed it back on and smiled at the mirror, uncaring that my reflection was a blank expression with two eye holes.

A slight knock came as my chamber door opened. It was Cyrus who—to his credit—appeared pleased to see me awake. "Is now a good time, Your Majesty?"

"Now is the only time I have left."

"Pardon?"

I snickered, grateful my mask hid my frown. "Tis a sad realm out there, General. I was unaware of how much I did not know until the truth barraged me from all angles. However, it would explain an interesting truth I learned about you. It would seem you are a man of many secrets."

"I knew this day would eventually come. Orion… Do you at least understand why?"

Understand what? Why did he use my old name? I was going to berate him about the rise of dust and cultists. If the rabbit hole went deeper than that, perhaps I would be better off in ignorance. Still, I didn't want to die without knowing. I had lived that way and, I assure you: it had not been a pleasant life. "It's not the why that concerns me, but the how. How could you? After everything we have been through?"

My general looked down. Whatever my lies had done to this man appeared to have wounded him. "I loved your father, but he was wrong. Even knowing what I do now, I knew he was wrong. I just…never expected your mother to respond so violently after I warned her. She was a gentle woman. I didn't think she had it in her."

I could not remember the last time I had laughed so hard. So

Cyrus had warned Mother about my father's plans to murder me, leading to Father's death. What a hilarious turn of events.

"Oh Mute, I fail to see the humor in such things. They both loved you in their unique ways. Do not tarnish their memory with laughter."

"I only intended to inquire about dust. The rest is…quite surprising."

"Ah." The lingering silence was beautiful. It was a natural lack of sound, more pure than the one triggered by my favorite word. Eventually, Cyrus said, "Do you at least understand that dust is more valuable than gold? It's a tax they willingly pay with blood. Balewind could never function without it."

"What is the correlation with the cultists? Have we funded our own demise?"

"They make the drug better. More addictive. We can't figure it out. Something from Ganfren, a cheaper, more dangerous substitute. It was a mistake to parley with them. I'll admit that."

Parley with them? Oh, dear. Looking back, I had been too harsh on ignorance. There was a joy to not knowing how the wheels of life turned. As it turns out, misery is the magical stone in which empires are built and maintained. I had done my part and then some. I had become the unknowing architect of woe. "It stops now."

"What? No! Mute, with all the unrest, we cannot simply stop funding the military. I understand. I get it. This is terrible, nasty business, but it's the way of the world. Do you wish to hear your father's final words to me? The words that haunt me every time I try to sleep? 'Close your ears to reason and you'll hear nothing but chaos.'"

I smiled. It did sound like Father. Sad, that he never felt the need to offer me his wisdom. "Maybe. Or perhaps I'll hear nothing at all. Stop the dust, no matter the consequences. You have your orders."

"No."

"Please don't make me explain how orders work to a general."

"Such an order would be impossible to carry out. I couldn't comply if you threatened to hang me. Your Majesty, I wield no magic, divine or otherwise. I cannot simply snap my fingers and solve the problems of our kingdom. If dust is no longer an option, I shall hand in my sword and resign. I cannot run Balewind on miracles and hope."

"Then you are dismissed." I walked over and embraced him, begging my eyes not to fixate on the pure agony on his face. "Leave this kingdom, knowing you served my family with honor. Thank you for everything, Cyrus. This is the closest I can come to repaying you. Tomorrow…will be a fine day for grave diggers."

He hesitated. Even through my mask I saw the flicker of hope in his eyes. I may as well have offered him heaven. "Then…I must depart? At once?"

"Immediately," I said, my voice cracking from the pain. At least Cyrus would survive. Apparently, I had only made it this far because of him. Such a debt could never be repaid. Best I could do was die and leave him out of it.

I was hoping he would say something poetic before he left. Instead, he saluted and rushed out the door. If you can believe it, I felt relief more than anything else. I would die tomorrow and the choice was no longer my own. For now, I was alone with my thoughts.

Ah, time may pass but some things never change. To be alone with my thoughts was just another form of being alone.

CHAPTER 12

SILENT ALMIGHTY

h oh, this chapter is named after the title of the book. That's probably a bad sign, or perhaps I'm simply overthinking things. I miss being naive. It's an underrated feeling. I miss staring into the mirror as a child, not understanding who or what was staring back. That blanket-like warmth of believing everything would work out in the end. That great times were soon upon me, as soon as I figured it all out.

Great times were not upon me. Simply speaking, I knew too much. I knew Deaf would accept my challenge. I knew most of my guards had fled with Cyrus—to where, I never found out. I knew today would be the last day of my life. Knowledge is said to be the grandest of pursuits, the glorious road to enlightenment and peace. Let me tell you, knowledge is a disease.

It probably goes without saying that I couldn't sleep last night. The guilt over dust's role in my reign was more powerful than I anticipated. The guilt over Merrick. The guilt over Dorothy. There is no cure for the disease of knowledge, save the man who just opened my throne room door. I could barely see him through the tint of moonlight, but the mask was unmistakable. It was Deaf. Lord Deaf, as he preferred. He had come to claim my kingdom. He had come to cleanse my filth.

He had come to take my life.

Looking back, I think life is just a thing that occurs before we die. A self-made journey of sorts, a disheveled road where most of the stones are a sorry combination of ignorance and poor judgment. The only path to heaven was the one that passed me by. I never saw it behind me but I knew it was gone. Sorry, I know I'm rambling. But it's a strange thing to write your own death, particularly in the past tense.

"You came," I said, which probably wasn't necessary as Deaf stood in the middle of my throne room. To his credit, he was alone.

"Where is my family?"

"Coralie!" I yelled, trying to make my voice louder than the outside thunder. She shuffled out from the room behind my throne, with little Norah at her side. To my surprise, they were wise enough not to speak. Coralie didn't even look in my direction. I couldn't say the same for Norah. She stared through me in a way that I swear meant pity. I don't know why. Never had the opportunity to ask.

"Noah!" the girl yelled. She rushed up and hugged her brother's leg. I don't think she was old enough to understand why he didn't hug her back. Deaf was anxious, probably wondering why I had lived up to my end of the bargain. It would have been the easiest trap ever laid, and instead, I did nothing. If knowledge was a disease, Deaf would remain pure. He was too driven and angry to understand how someone could grow tired of being alive.

Deaf drew his dagger. It was larger and encrusted with diamonds at the hilt, far grander than the one I had seen in his place of worship. Not very practical, but I respected the showmanship of it. "So you have decided to die with honor. I'll admit, that surprises me. You are a strange man, Lord Mute. I will speak truthfully: the history books shall not remember you fondly.

I can wield lies and deception with ease, but there is no force powerful enough to repair your reign."

I shrugged my shoulders. "Just tell them the truth. Let my people come to their own conclusions. They may surprise you, Lord Deaf. Besides, history may view me more favorably after a few years of you."

"I care not what they feel. The only relevant factor is what they believe. And as soon as our business here is concluded, belief will never be a choice again." Deaf did a slight chuckle before laughing. "It could have been you. I am forever grateful that it wasn't. Do you not feel Lepock's love? His glory? His *power*?"

"I feel his lingering silence. I have felt it since Mother's departure. It's why I pity you. No matter which dagger finds blood here tonight, there is no victory to be had. Lepock cares nothing for us. We are simply pawns at the front of the board, gifted with nothing more than a dagger and a crown of lies."

Deaf began his ascent up the stairs. Hopefully, I struck a nerve. If I couldn't defeat him in melee combat, I could die happier knowing that I hurt his feelings. "Stay, Norah," Deaf yelled, never taking his eyes off me. "I want you to watch. You are too young to understand the importance of faith. Let the death of this false king serve as your first and final reminder."

I was impressed at how quickly Deaf rushed up the stairs, but less impressed at how foolish his strategy was. It's important to respect the high ground. I doubt he expected my kick as he made the final step. It knocked him off balance, enough to where he fell down the stairs just as quickly as he had risen. I shouldn't have hesitated. Every moment in battle is precious. I rushed down after him, resisting the temptation to throw my full body weight while he was still on the ground. To his credit, he never let go of the dagger. It would have been nice to know his background. At the time, I assumed he had very little battle experience. Seemed like the type to yell out orders and claim all the glory after the battle was over.

That assumption had not been correct.

Deaf kicked me right below the knee, sending me to the ground at a very unfortunate angle. I screamed, and I don't care if such a thing cost my dignity—it hurt, and it hurt a lot. By instinct, I ignored the pain and rolled a few feet over to my left, then forced myself up on my good leg first. Fortunately, my bad leg still worked. It would be less responsive than normal, but I could live with that.

Deaf had the same idea. He recovered on the opposite side, then immediately rushed over. To be honest, I was tired of this man rushing me, so I rushed him back. I was nowhere near as fast, but it didn't really matter as we were rushing in the same direction. His dagger swing was wild. I barely got my blade up in time to block my head from getting carved off. He swung again before I could regain myself, slashing across my mask. It didn't exactly hurt, but it wounded my pride.

So I tackled him. It wasn't pretty, it wasn't technical, but it got us off our legs and back onto the ground. There, his speed didn't matter. We were two masked fools, punching each other in various locations despite our masks and heavy coats. He must have realized the absurdity of it as he finally grabbed me by the throat and bore his weight on my chest. I didn't have the ability to break free. I punched, grabbed, I even clawed, but nothing worked. If I survived this ordeal, I swore my next nemesis would be a smaller man who didn't wear a mask.

I punched his chest where his heart was, over and over, but nothing happened. I don't know if my attacks caused him pain. I hope they did, though power was probably lacking as my body lost air. Blurred vision is never a good sign. I saw several Deafs, who were all grasping my neck.

There had to be another way. I grasped all around me, looking for a rock, a blade, a gold coin, anything. Anything! My left hand found something. I don't know what it was but I swung it up with every remaining ounce of strength.

I could only laugh. It was Deaf's own dagger, and it stabbed straight through his mask. It hit something—I assumed flesh, but whatever it was, it was enough. His grip lost strength. Seeing my moment, I tore the blade down, tearing off an amalgamation of mask and flesh. It was always better to inflict pain on others than experience it myself. Deaf screamed and let go.

My vision returned. My heart beat. My focus was invincible. With his dagger still in my hand, I rose from the ground and observed him like an apex predator. Blood poured down his jaw as he wheezed in pain. It felt *wrong* that I would win. I didn't want to win! I wanted peace, wanted slumber. Instead, I was destined to be the king with no army or general.

I really didn't know what to do. Winning was never part of the plan. I kicked him in the ribs. It didn't feel like a clean blow but Deaf managed a low-pitched scream from the ground. He struggled to breathe. What a pity. I kicked him again. Again. A few more times, reveling in the adrenaline that came after each strike. Absurd. Completely absurd. Are you telling me that I won? That I defeated the twenty-five-year-old man in a battle to the death?

Tomorrow would be unfortunate. I would need to hire a new general—at a much lower rate. My army needed rebuilding. These heretics needed to hang. There was a lot of work to do. I didn't even know where to—

"Stop it!" Norah yelled, rushing in front of her fallen brother. She stretched her arms out in a protective gesture as if that would do something. "Leave my brother alone!"

The way she looked at me was unfortunate. I swear, I was growing tired of women of all shapes, colors, and ages looking at me like I was a monster. I wasn't. I really wasn't. "Sorry, deary. As I mentioned, two kings is one too many. Take care of your mother.

If you both leave here by tomorrow, I vow to never search for you. It's not heaven, but it's the only thing I can offer."

I could practically watch her tiny mind search for options. Hopefully, it wouldn't take her too long to realize there was only one. A fair one, in hindsight, a—

"Monster," she whispered, her eyes looking away.

That word. How I hated that word. How I despised that word. I knelt to her height and took off my mask. "Look at me, child. Do I look like a monster to you?"

"You're going to hurt my brother and mommy. So many monsters have already hurt them. Why does everyone hate my family? Why do my prayers never come true?"

I smiled for a moment before remembering she could see it. I patted her on the shoulder and rose. "Monsters create other monsters. The only heroes in this realm are the ones who craft their suffering into a shield to protect others."

"Like you?" asked Norah.

I thought back to my family. I thought back to Dorothy. I thought back to the hundreds, if not thousands, of dust addicts. "Heavens no. My sins are on a scale that rivals Lepock himself. Sorry Norah, I cannot stop this world from creating monsters. But perhaps…one time…I can answer your prayers. When you grow old, remember my mercy. Remember that there is always an opportunity to do better." I handed her my mask and said, "Save our realm from the Silent Almighty. Succeed, where I have failed." I threw my dagger on the ground and walked away.

"Why?" asked Coralie, emerging from the shadows. "Why didn't you kill him?"

"For Norah. Your son is already lost, but there is hope in the girl. I would not dare take that away from her. Farewell, Coralie. You shall never see me again."

"Thank you," Coralie whispered, and I think she meant it.

As I left my throne room for the final time, Norah yelled out,

"My prayers have been answered! Thank you, Lord Mute! I shall never forget your kindness! You are a good man and I love you! All hail the Silent Almighty! Sing his praise! For he has given us mercy! All hail the Silent Almighty! All hail the Silent Almighty!" She kept yelling, to the point where I was tempted to call upon my silence. To hear her credit my empathy to Lepock was a defeat worse than anything Deaf could have done to me. I had done so much wrong in my life, so many terrible things with violence, but was mercy just as terrible? I wouldn't know. Call me a coward, but I didn't care to find out. Finally, in the eyes of this little girl, I was the hero of the story. Finally, I had finally chosen peace.

And in doing so, I had made the realm worse off forever.

EPILOGUE

CONTENT

ontent is a fascinating word. In all my years, I have asked countless people how their day was going in the attempt at banal conversation. Funny, how no one ever answered content. And why not? No one ever said terrible. No one ever said wonderful. It's odd really, how our dreams deteriorate with time. I wanted to be God. When that failed, I wanted to be king. I eventually settled on something that wasn't Mute. Hopefully, purgatory wasn't filled with people like me. I hoped it wasn't filled with anyone at all really. I just wanted to rest. To dream. To wonder.

I just wanted to be happy

More people should aim for content. Honestly, it's the only dream that ever comes true. That half frown, half smirk, where life isn't grand but the worst days of our life have already passed. I had failed in my time as king. I had failed in my time as a brother. I had failed in my time as a son. Admitting such things brought peace. Admitting that such catastrophes were now other people's problems truly made me content.

I glance at my book one last time before sliding it into the dresser of my room at the inn. *Silent Almighty* seems like a reasonable title. Someone will find it eventually and rate it three out of five stars, which is the rating that sums up my life thus far. Hopefully by then, the realm will be a better place. They can analyze my decisions and determine that I am, in fact, not a monster. If I had to guess, I am simply a man addicted to terrible decisions. If there is an opportunity to make the realm worse off, I find it. I always find it. It's like a cruel sense of genius. A madman's prerogative.

As of today, kind judgment is unlikely. Deaf's forces have seized complete control over Balewind. Hangings occur daily, and dust is as common as water. I should have killed him. I know that now. I'm sure my family is laughing from the grave at my ability to take something as beautiful as compassion and turn it into a dystopian catalyst.

There are rumors that King Mute still lives. Like most simple offenses, such words are punishable by death. It barely concerns me. Without my mask, I am no one, and I am fully content with that. Purpose had finally come by pretending to be someone else. I walk down the stairs, to the front of the inn, and I smile at the innkeeper. I ensure to pay him only in copper to avoid suspicion. He smiles back, which is nice, but nothing I'll remember an hour from now.

My ship is there on the bay. A quaint little thing—enough to carry ten or so passengers. I had waited five months before booking passage. Time is always the death of security, and today would be no different. My quarters are cramped, hot, and a bizarre scent fills the room. Tis rare to smell something for the first time after thirty-six years. The discovery is nothing dreadful, nothing enthralling, but just enough to make me content.

I lean back on my bed and sigh. My bed is uncomfortable, and I do not care in the slightest. All that matters is my departure. Off to the kingdom of Roppa to start anew, all the way on the other side of the realm. A strange land, where the inhabitants worship all sorts of gods, from bear gods, to spider gods, to angelic soldier gods. Oh my! I know nothing about any of them, and such a profound lack of knowledge makes my heart beat at a content rhythm.

The ship takes sail. I admit the rocking makes me un-comfortable. I take a sip of water and leave my quarters. It's probably unwise to watch the waves crash while feeling queasy, though the ocean breeze brings a tranquil calm. My grip tightens on the railing as we hit a wave. I shouldn't be out here. Safety would be within my quarters, and I always cling to safety. At least the captain is outside. A great time to make conversation.

"A fair morning to sail, my lord," I say to the captain. He does not respond.

And I cannot tell you how content that makes me feel.

THANK YOU FOR READING!

If you happened to enjoy this novella, feel free to pick up my epic fantasy trilogy: The Legacy of Boulom, featuring Platinum Tinted Darkness, Tears of the Maelstrom, and Age of Arrogance.

Willow Wraith Press is a collective of nerds who write the types of books we want to read. If you have enjoyed this book, please check out the other Willow Wraiths.

Dewey Conway & Bill Adams:

The Tenacious Tale of Tanna the Tendersword

Bill Adams:

The Godsblood Tragedy

Andrew D. Meredith:

Deathless Beast
Bone Shroud
Gloves of Eons

Thrice
Four Scored

Quaint Creatures: Magical & Mundane

Michael Roberti:

The Traitors We Are
A Grave for Us All
The Revenge of Thousands

Timothy Wolff:

Platinum Tinted Darkness
Tears of the Maelstrom
Age of Arrogance

The Whisper that Replaced God
Silent Almighty

MEET THE AUTHOR

Timothy Wolff lives in Long Island, New York, and holds a Master's degree in economics and a career in finance. Such a life has taught him the price of everything but the value of nothing. He enjoys pizza bagels, scotch, karaoke, oxford commas, and spending the day with family and friends. The obvious culmination of the past thirty-six years was to write a 400+ page fantasy novel where a drunk teams up with a swordsman, two mages, and lizard-people to oppose god. Why do we write these in the third person?

Strength without honor—is chaos!

He can be reached at:

@TimWolffAuthor on Twitter, X, or whatever the hell the site is called by the time this book is published.

Timwolffauthor on Instagram/Threads/BlueSky

timwolffauthor@gmail.com

THANKS, ACKNOWLEDGEMENTS, ETC.

I had no intentions of writing this book until I started to write this book. Mute will return in *Requiem of Dice*, a stand-alone full length novel set in the same world but on a different continent. I'm aiming for late 2025 or worse-case, early 2026. The *Platinum Tinted Darkness* relaunch is set for February 2025 and after that, I have no idea.

As always, first thanks go to my immediate family of Joan, Larry, and Danny, who have always been super supportive despite not being fans of the fantasy genre. I usually don't thank my extended family in fear of missing someone, but I do want to extend a special thanks to my cousin, Kelsey.

Special thanks to my editor, Jon Oliver, who has fixed the horrors of my comma and semicolon usage for four five books now, and overall is an awesome dude.

Anyone who follows my work probably knows all my covers are done by Alejandro Colucci. Aside from being one of the nicest people I've ever worked with, his ability to turn my unhinged descriptions into something amazing is a skill I will forever envy.

The indie fantasy community has been amazing. I always found "no one writes alone" to be a cliché, but I now swear by it. Writing can be brutal at times. Sometimes the words don't come. Sometimes the words come and they are very bad. The community is a blessing, and I am forever grateful for all the people I met in the past two years. Forgive me skipping names, but I don't want to miss anyone. I think you know who you are.